6 JUN 2019

5/3/22

HENDON LIE

KT-574-467

2629

Wizard

Steve Barlow and Steve Skidmore

Illustrated by Jack Lawrence

30131 05357958 4

LONDON BOROUGH OF BARNET

Franklin Watts
First published in Great Britain in 2015 by The Watts Publishing Group

Text © Steve Barlow and Steve Skidmore 2015
Illustrations by Jack Lawrence © Franklin Watts 2015
The "2Steves" illustration by Paul Davidson
used by kind permission of Orchard Books

The authors and illustrator have asserted their rights in
accordance with the Copyright, Designs and Patents Act, 1988.

All rights reserved.

PB ISBN 978 1 4451 3958 6
ebook ISBN 978 1 4451 3961 6
Library ebook ISBN 978 1 4451 3962 3

1 3 5 7 9 10 8 6 4 2

Printed in Great Britain

MIX
Paper from
responsible sources
FSC
www.fsc.org
FSC® C104740

Franklin Watts
An imprint of
Hachette Children's Group
Part of The Watts Publishing Group
Carmelite House
50 Victoria Embankment
London EC4Y 0DZ

An Hachette UK Company
www.hachette.co.uk

www.franklinwatts.co.uk

How to be a hero

This book is not like others you have read. This is a choose-your-own-destiny book where YOU are the hero of this adventure.

Each section of this book is numbered. At the end of most sections, you will have to make a choice. Each choice will take you to a different section of the book.

If you choose correctly, you will succeed. But be careful. If you make a bad choice, you may have to start the adventure again. If this happens, make sure you learn from your mistake!

Go to the next page to start your adventure. And remember, don't be a zero, be a hero!

You are an apprentice wizard living in Nine Mountains kingdom. You have been studying magic for many years under the guidance of your master, Magir the Wise. He is an old and powerful wizard. You have learnt well and use your magic for good.

The kingdom is ruled by King Oswald the Great and Queen Lana the Blessed. Their baby son, Prince Bron, is the heir to the kingdom. Many different creatures live in the Nine Mountains. Dwarfs, trolls and other amazing beasts live in peace with humans.

All is well in the kingdom, but evil is never far away...

Now go to 1.

1

Early one autumn morning you are summoned to King Oswald's throne room. You enter and see Magir looking grim-faced. The king and queen are in tears.

Magir begins to speak. "During the night Prince Bron was taken from his cradle. This was left in his place." He holds up an ice-white crystal.

"It's a message crystal," you say.

Magir nods. "From the Witch Queen of the White Mountain." He strikes the crystal with his hand. There is a flash of light and an image of the Witch Queen emerges. It begins to speak.

"Hear me, King and Queen. I have your son. In return for his life, I want to be ruler of the kingdom. You have until dawn tomorrow to agree to my demand." The image disappears.

"What has this got to do with me?" you ask.

King Oswald replies. "We want you

to find the prince and return him safely."

If you wish to undertake the quest immediately, go to 14.

If you wish to find out more, go to 47.

2

You point Greystaff at the cat. "Reveal!" There is a flash of light and the cat turns into the baby prince. You suddenly realise the horror of the situation. You spin around to see the Witch Queen emerge from the cradle. She was disguised as the baby!

"Destructo!" you cry and send an ice blast at the Witch Queen. She avoids your attack and sends a sheet of flame at you, just before she turns into a dragon! You dodge the fire, but it hits the walls of the cottage and sets them alight. You hear the prince cry — he is trapped behind the fire!

To rescue the prince, go to 45.

To continue to fight the Witch Queen, go to 31.

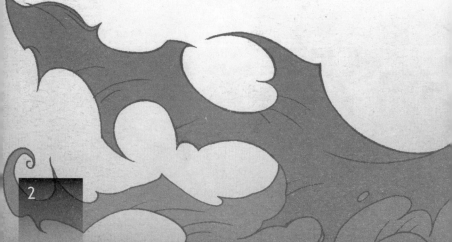

3

You hold out Greystaff. "Veritas!" you cry. "Tell me truly. Are you what you appear to be?"

The nymph scowls. "Your magic will not work against me. You do not trust me and so I will not trust you." She disappears under the water, leaving you wondering who she was.

Go to 10.

4

"We don't have much time, so I will choose Windrunner," you say. Magir nods in agreement.

You pack provisions for the journey and leave the castle heading north.

Windrunner is fast and you soon arrive at the edge of the Great Forest. It is still light, but you know that the forest is dangerous at night.

To continue into the forest, go to 41.
To find somewhere to rest, go to 36.

5

"How will I find the Witch's lair when I'm in the Caverns of Doom?" you ask.

"Look for the Giant's Hand," the nymph replies. "Go to the middle tower. You will find the Witch Queen there, but be careful, and trust your magical powers." The nymph disappears beneath the water.

Go to 10.

6

You point Greystaff at the trees. "Stasis!" you cry. Stars fly from the staff, covering the trees and lighting up the forest. Immediately the trees stop moving. Your paralysis spell has worked!

You urge Windrunner forward and she speeds through the trees.

As you leave the Great Forest, the moon lights up your destination — the White Mountain.

Go to 46.

7

You move towards the sound. Suddenly the walls explode as a huge creature bursts through the rock and heads towards you.

If you want to escape, go to 48.
To face your enemy, go to 18.

8

You set off on foot heading north. You walk for many hours. It is a hard journey and night has fallen by the time you reach the Great Forest.

To enter the forest, go to 44.
To find somewhere to rest instead, go to 36.

9

Before you can question Ukin, there is a noise above you. You look up to see a huge flying scorpion heading towards you!

It screeches and shoots a stream of venomous poison at you from its tail. You leap out of the way, but the poison hits Ukin, and he drops to the ground.

"Destructo!" You send a fireball at the scorpion. The creature plummets to the ground in flames.

If the nymph told you about the Giant's Hand, go to 40.
If she didn't, go to 37.

10

You leave the pool and head towards the White Mountain.

Suddenly the sky darkens as a black cloud forms above you. It begins to move towards you. You peer into the cloud and your blood turns to ice. It is a swarm of vulture bats!

If you wish to attack them, go to 43.
To cast a spell of invisibility on yourself, go to 32.

11

You point Greystaff at the old woman. "Show your true self!" you command.

There is a flash of light as the woman is caught in your magical spell. She transforms

into what she truly is — a wolfhag! It snarls at you, but is powerless to move.

"Begone forever!" you cry. There is another flash of light and the wolfhag vanishes. You decide to leave.

If you were riding Stormcloud, go to 28.
If you were riding Windrunner, go to 41.
If you were making the journey on foot, go to 44.

12

You wake up to find an ugly creature standing in front of you. It is a cave troll!

"So, you have finally woken," it snarls. "Good. It's dinner time. And you're my dessert," it says.

The creature moves towards you.

Go to 23.

13

You continue following the course of the river. The cliffs of the valley get steeper and your horse is tiring. You see a small cave in one of the cliffs and decide to rest there.

"Illuminos," you command. Greystaff emits a steady flame, providing warmth and light. You settle down to rest.

Soon after you hear a noise coming from deep within the cave.

If you want to leave the cave, go to 48.
If you wish to explore the cave, go to 7.

14

"Of course I will do this task," you say. "I will leave immediately!"

"Do not be so foolish," snaps Magir. "You know nothing of the quest. You need to know more."

You realise that your master is right.

Don't be so hasty. Go to 47.

15

As you scramble to the bank the water-serpent's mouth snaps down on your arm and you let out a cry.

Go to 23.

16

As the rocks crash down you hold out Greystaff and cry, "Reveal!"

There is a flash of light and the tower disappears. You find yourself standing outside a cottage in a forest glade. You realise that the tower was an illusion and this is the real lair of the Witch Queen!

You enter the cottage and see a cat stretched out in front of the fire and the prince lying in a cradle.

If you wish to pick up the prince, go to 27.

If you'd prefer to put a spell on the cat, go to 2.

17

You place Greystaff against Stormcloud's head. "Forward!" you command.

The horse obeys.

As you continue down the track, there is a blast of wind. Leaves swirl about you, smothering you and the horse. Trees begin to close in on you. The forest has come to life!

"Faster," you urge Stormcloud, but at that moment a tree branch smashes into you and knocks you to the ground.

To fight the trees, go to 30.
To try to escape, go to 23.

18

The creature charges towards you. It is a cave troll!

"Sleep!" you cry. A cloud of smoke hits the cave troll and it drops to the ground. Your relief is short-lived as more trolls appear. You are badly outnumbered!

Go to 23.

19

"The journey will be hard, so I will choose Stormcloud," you say.

You pack provisions for the journey and leave the castle, heading north. Although Stormcloud is strong, he is not fast and the sun is setting as you reach the Great Forest.

If you wish to enter the forest, go to 28.

To find somewhere to rest, go to 36.

20

You push at the gates. Suddenly a huge black spider scuttles across the gates and grabs hold of you. Before you can react it sinks its fangs into your back. Its venom enters your body, slowly freezing your limbs.

"Antidos!" you cry. The spell acts as a cure to the venom. But at that moment more spiders appear. You know you cannot survive against this many!

Go to 23.

21

You leap back onto Windrunner and urge her forwards. She takes off down the track.

The trees thrash at you, but you have chosen your horse well. She zigzags between the trees that try to block your path.

However, there are hundreds of trees. They gather together, trapping you and Windrunner.

To fight the trees, go to 30.
To cast a spell to clear the way, go to 6.

22

"I don't think so," you reply. "You will take me to where the prince is being held. You will use secret ways and avoid the Witch Queen's servants."

You point Greystaff at the cave troll. "Obey."

The spell forms and Ukin leads you through the cavern's secret tunnels. Eventually, you see light ahead where there is an outcrop of rock with five towers.

"What is this place?" you ask.

Ukin replies. "The Giant's Hand."

To put Ukin to sleep, go to 29.
To ask him more questions, go to 9.

Desperately, you reach for the amulet and cry, "Return!"

There is a swirl of light as you pass through time and space. You find yourself back in your master's spell room.

Magir stares at you. "You made a wrong choice. Begin your quest again, and this time choose wisely!"

If you wish to begin your journey on foot, go to 8.

If you wish to begin your journey on horseback, go to 39.

24

You hide behind a rock. "Dark light," you command. The light from Greystaff dims and produces a green glow.

The scraping stops and a huge creature emerges from the wall. It turns towards you, sniffing at the air. It knows you are here!

You stand up and face your enemy.

If you want to cast a spell to put the creature to sleep, go to 18.

If you want to cast a spell to put it under your control, go to 34.

25

"I will do what you ask," you reply.

Magir hands you an amulet. "This is the Amulet of Protection. If you find yourself in peril and cannot escape, place your hand on it and say the word 'return'. The power of the amulet's magic will bring you back to this time and place, where you may begin your quest again."

He also hands you his magician's staff. "This is Greystaff — it has great power. It will make your magic more powerful. Use it wisely when casting your spells. Now you must begin your journey. Time is running out."

If you wish to begin your journey on foot, go to 8.

If you wish to begin your journey on horseback, go to 39.

26

"To me, Greystaff!" you command. The staff flies through the air into your hand and you point it at the water-serpent. "Destructo!"

There is a flash of light and an explosion as the creature vanishes. Steam rises from the pool as you drag yourself out.

As you lie on the bank you hear a voice. "Thank you."

You look up and see a water nymph in the pool.

If you wish to talk to the creature, go to 38.

If you want to make sure the creature is what she appears to be, go to 3.

You put Greystaff on the table, reach into the cradle and pick up the prince. As you do so, the baby transforms into the Witch Queen!

She laughs manically before changing once again. This time her body turns into a giant snake, which she wraps around you. She begins to squeeze the life out of you.

Go to 23.

28

You guide Stormcloud through the forest. It is dark, so you say "Illuminos!" to light up your staff and help you to see your way.

Suddenly, Stormcloud stops and stamps his foot, refusing to continue. You peer into the trees, but can see nothing.

If you want to get off Stormcloud and walk down the track, go to 44.

If you want to force Stormcloud to continue, go to 17.

29

You point Greystaff at Ukin.

But before you can cast the sleep spell, he cries, "Brothers, help me!"

More cave trolls suddenly appear. They see you and charge. You are outnumbered!

Go to 23.

30

You point your staff. "Vulcanas!" you cry. A flame shoots from Greystaff and hits a great fir tree, setting it alight. It roars and crashes to the ground.

More trees join the attack. Time and again you send sheets of fire towards them. It seems that the whole forest is burning!

Suddenly you realise that you have made a great mistake. You are trapped by the burning trees!

Go to 23.

31

You send another ice blast at the dragon, but the beast dodges out of the way.

Without warning the burning roof collapses, burying you underneath its wooden beams. The dragon picks up the prince, blasts its way through the wall and flies away. The fire burns around you.

Go to 23.

32

"Invisibilis!" you cry.

You turn invisible, but the bats are still

heading towards you! You realise that you have made a mistake — bats don't need eyes to find you. They can see by using sound waves.

Before you can react, the swarm hits you, knocking Greystaff from your hand. The vulture bats attack you and Windrunner with their talons and razor-sharp teeth.

Go to 23.

33

"I am not worthy of this task," you say. "Find someone else."

"I can order you to do this," says the king angrily.

"Wait, husband," says the queen. She turns to you. "You are my son's only hope. I beg you."

You realise that you have to undertake this quest, despite the danger.

Go to 25.

34

"Captivo," you command. A stream of light shoots from Greystaff and surrounds the creature. It stops and is unable to move.

"What are you?" you ask.

Your magic forces it to reply. "I am Ukin, a cave troll, and a servant of the Witch Queen. She knows you are coming. You will fail in your quest."

If you want to make the troll take you to the prince, go to 22.

If you want to put the creature to sleep, go to 29.

35

You know you have to go high into the
White Mountain to find the Spider Gates,
so you head towards the high pass.

After many hours of travelling, you see
two great gates set into the mountainside.
These are the Spider Gates, the entrance
to the Caverns of Doom.

You will not be able to take Windrunner
into the caverns, so you dismount and tell
her to head home. She turns and gallops
off. You are on your own.

To enter the cavern, go to 20.

**If you wish to make sure all is safe first,
go to 42.**

36

You see a woodcutter's cabin nestled
between the trees. You make your way to
it and knock on the door.

An old woman opens it. "How can I help
you, deary?" she asks.

You explain who you are and ask for a

room for the night. She agrees and invites you in. She offers you food.

If you wish to accept her food, go to 49.
If you wish to make sure it is safe to stay, go to 11.

You decide to cast a spell to reveal which tower you should head towards.

"Reveal!" you command. Nothing happens. The witch must have placed a protection spell around her lair.

As you consider what to do, the earth begins to shake violently. You spin around to see a rock giant holding a huge stone club.

It swings the club and it crashes down, sending you sprawling. Greystaff spins out of your grasp.

The rock giant stands over you and raises his club to strike again.

Go to 23.

38

"Why do you thank me?" you ask.

"Because you have released me from the evil curse of the Witch Queen. She turned me into the water-serpent many years ago. But now I am free."

You tell the nymph of your quest.

"Then I can help," she says. "To reach the Witch Queen's lair, you must pass through the Spider Gates high in the White Mountain and enter the Caverns of Doom. Good luck."

If you wish to ask her more questions, go to 5.

If you wish to head up to the mountain, go to 10.

You head to the castle stables with Magir. He points to two horses. "Which one will you choose?" he asks. "Windrunner is the fastest horse in the kingdom. Stormcloud is the strongest."

To choose Windrunner, go to 4.
To choose Stormcloud, go to 19.

40

You remember that the nymph said to go to the middle tower and trust your magic. You cast a spell of invisibility around you and make your way to the witch's lair.

As you get closer the gates to the tower open. You trust your spell of invisibility and enter a courtyard. The gates crash shut behind you. The noise vibrates the air, making your head spin. The tower begins to rock. Walls begin to crumble and huge stones crash down.

If you wish to get out of the tower, go to 23.

If you want to cast a spell, go to 16.

41

Windrunner speeds down the forest track. Eventually, the sun sets and the forest is filled with strange noises as the creatures of the night begin to wake.

A strong wind blows and the trees begin to sway. Something ahead of you catches your eye. You look carefully. The trees aren't just swaying, they are moving towards you. The forest has come alive!

As you urge Windrunner forwards, a giant fir tree uproots itself and steps into your path. Windrunner rears up, causing you to fall from your saddle. The trees move in for the kill!

To try to escape on Windrunner, go to 21.

To fight the trees, go to 30.

You hold up Greystaff. "Enemies reveal yourselves." A light surrounds the gate and a huge spider drops down in front of you, spinning on a silk line.

"Destructo!" you cry and blast it with a fireball. You leave the spider to burn and head through the gates into the caverns. Greystaff lights your way. As you move forward you hear a scraping noise ahead of you.

To investigate the noise, go to 7.
If you wish to hide, go to 24.

43

You spur Windrunner towards the incoming enemy. Pointing Greystaff you cry, "Destructo!" Fireballs shoot from the staff and explode in the middle of the swarm. The air is filled with ash.

The surviving bats break off their attack and fly back towards the mountain. The Witch Queen knows you are coming!

If the water nymph thanked you, go to 35.
If she didn't, go to 13.

44

As you make your way down the forest track, there is a sudden blast of wind. Leaves swirl around your body, almost choking you.

You hold out your staff, but before you can utter a spell, it is snatched from your grip by a tree branch. You peer through the whirlpool of leaves and see the trees walking towards you. They are alive! More branches grab hold of you and pin you down.

Go to 23.

45

"Aqua!" you command, and a flood of water pours from Greystaff, putting out the fire.

You pick up the prince, before pointing Greystaff at the dragon. "Be gone forever!" you command.

Stars pour out of Greystaff, engulfing the dragon. It tries to fight back, but your magic is too strong. There is a scream and then nothing as the beast turns to ash.

Holding Prince Bron to your chest, you reach for your amulet and cry, "Return!"

Go to 50.

46

You decide to follow the course of the river. In the moonlight you find yourself at a small pool. You dismount and kneel on the bank to fill your waterskin.

Suddenly there is a great roaring noise as a huge water-serpent bursts from the pool. Water crashes over your head and you fall into the pool. Your staff lies on the bank as the water-serpent heads towards you.

If you want to try to get out of the water, go to 15.

If you want to try to cast a spell, go to 26.

"But why not send the Royal Guards on this quest?" you ask.

"The Witch Queen can only be defeated by magic, not brute force," replies Magir.

You are puzzled. "So why me and not you, Master?"

"I am too old to travel," replies Magir. "You are young enough to journey north to the White Mountain, find the lair of the Witch Queen and rescue the prince. It will be dangerous, but the future of the kingdom depends on you."

If you wish to undertake the quest, go to 25.

If you think it sounds too dangerous, go to 33.

48

You hurry out, but run straight into a big rope net that stretches across the entrance. You drop Greystaff as the net tightens around you. You are trapped!

Before you can retrieve Greystaff or use the amulet, you feel a blow to the head and you pass out.

Go to 12.

49

You sit at a table and the old woman places a bowl of stew in front of you.

You begin to eat as the woman looks on. After the first few mouthfuls, you begin to feel dizzy. The food is drugged! You look up through dazed eyes and see the woman transform into a wolfhag!

The creature leaps towards you with its claws out and its mouth open, revealing rows of sharp teeth.

Go to 23.

50

There is a swirl of light and you find yourself back in the throne room of King Oswald and Queen Lana. The king and queen rush to you and take back their prince.

"How did you overcome the Witch?" asks the queen. You describe your adventures to her and the king.

"Thank you," says the king. "We are in your debt."

Magir steps forward. "Well done," he says. "The kingdom is rid of the Witch Queen forever. You did well."

"Thank you, Master," you reply.

Magir smiles. "Hah! I am no longer your master, and you are no longer an apprentice. You have proved yourself to be a brave wizard in your own right. You are a hero!"

Immortals

HERO

I HERO Quiz

Test yourself with this special quiz. It has been designed to see how much you remember about the book you've just read. Can you get all five answers right?

Download answer sheets from:

https://www.hachettechildrens.co.uk/ Teacher%27s%20Zone/non_fiction_ activity_sheets.page

Question 1

What is the name of the staff given to you by Magir?

A   Whitestaff

B   Staff of Protection

C   Greystaff

D   Goldstaff

Question 2

What is the name of the cave troll
who you find on the White Mountain?

A   Bron

B   Ukin

C   Lana

D   Magir

Question 3

Which sort of creature appears after you destroy the water-serpent?

A   a mermaid

B   a pixie

C   a fairy

D   a nymph

Question 4

What is the name of the amulet given to you by Magir?

A   Amulet of Protection

B   Amulet of Power

C   Greystaff

D   Amulet of Magic

Question 5

Who are you sent on a quest to defeat?

A   White Queen

B   Snow Queen

C   Witch Queen

D   Mountain Queen

About the 2Steves

"The 2Steves" are Britain's most popular writing double act for young people, specialising in comedy and adventure. They perform regularly in schools and libraries, and at festivals, taking the power of words and story to audiences of all ages.

Together they have written many books, including the *Crime Team* series. Find out what they've been up to at: **www.the2steves.net**

About the illustrator: Jack Lawrence

Jack Lawrence is a successful freelance comics illustrator, working on titles such as *A.T.O.M.*, Cartoon Network, *Doctor Who Adventures*, *2000 AD*, *Gogos Mega Metropolis* and *Spider-Man Tower of Power*. He also works as a freelance toy designer.

Jack lives in Maidstone in Kent with his partner and two cats.

Have you completed the I HERO Quests?

Battle with aliens in Tyranno Quest:

AIR BLAST
978 1 4451 0875 9 pb
978 1 4451 1345 6 ebook

FIRE STORM
978 1 4451 0876 6 pb
978 1 4451 1346 3 ebook

ICE STRIKE
978 1 4451 0877 3 pb
978 1 4451 1347 0 ebook

EARTH ATTACK
978 1 4451 0878 0 pb
978 1 4451 1348 7 ebook

Defeat the Red Queen in Blood Crown Quest:

SANDS OF BLOOD
978 1 4451 1499 6 pb
978 1 4451 1503 0 ebook

DRAGON MOUNTAIN
978 1 4451 1500 9 pb
978 1 4451 1504 7 ebook

DEMON SEA
978 1 4451 1501 6 pb
978 1 4451 1505 4 ebook

CITY OF THE DEAD
978 1 4451 1502 3 pb
978 1 4451 1506 1 ebook

Save planet Earth in Atlantis Quest:

MENACE FROM THE DEEP
978 1 4451 2867 2 pb
978 1 4451 2868 9 ebook

OCEAN ALLIANCE
978 1 4451 2870 2 pb
978 1 4451 2871 9 ebook

BATTLE FOR THE SEAS
978 1 4451 2876 4 pb
978 1 4451 2877 1 ebook

ATLANTIS ASSAULT
978 1 4451 2873 3 pb
978 1 4451 2874 0 ebook

Also by the 2Steves...

978 0 7496 9283 4 pb
978 1 4451 0843 8 eBook

A millionaire is found at his luxury island home – dead! But no one can work out how he died. You must get to Skull Island and solve the mystery before his killer escapes.

978 0 7496 9284 1 pb
978 1 4451 0844 5 eBook

The daughter of a Hong Kong businessman has been kidnapped. You must find her, but who took her and why? You must crack the case, before it's too late!

978 0 7496 9286 5 pb
978 1 4451 0845 2 eBook

You must solve the clues to stop a terrorist attack in London. But who is planning the attack, and when will it take place? It's a race against time!

978 0 7496 9285 8 pb
978 1 4451 0846 9 eBook

An armoured convoy has been attacked in Moscow and hundreds of gold bars stolen. But who was behind the raid, and where is the gold? Get the clues - get the gold.